# Princess Ponies

## An Amazing Rescue

## The Princess Ponies series

# Princess Ponies

## An Amazing Rescue

## CHLOE RYDER

BLOOMSBURY

NEW YORK  LONDON  NEW DELHI  SYDNEY

First published in Great Britain in August 2013 by Bloomsbury Publishing Plc
Published in the United States of America in January 2015
by Bloomsbury Children's Books
www.bloomsbury.com

Bloomsbury is a registered trademark of Bloomsbury Publishing Plc

For information about permission to reproduce selections from this book, write to
Permissions, Bloomsbury Children's Books, 1385 Broadway, New York, New York 10018
Bloomsbury books may be purchased for business or promotional use. For information on
bulk purchases please contact Macmillan Corporate and Premium Sales Department at
specialmarkets@macmillan.com

Library of Congress Cataloging-in-Publication Data
Ryder, Chloe.
An amazing rescue / Chloe Ryder.
pages      cm.      — (Princess ponies ; 5)
Summary: While searching for the remaining golden horseshoes needed to keep
the island of Chevalia enchanted, Pippa and princess pony Stardust enter the
Wild Forest and meet Princess Cloud, a wild pony with a tempting invitation.
ISBN 978-1-61963-403-9 (paperback) • ISBN 978-1-61963-404-6 (e-book)
[1. Ponies—Fiction. 2. Magic—Fiction. 3. Princesses—Fiction.] I. Title.
PZ7.R95898Am 2014      [Fic]—dc23      2014005940

Typeset by Hewer Text UK Ltd, Edinburgh
Printed in China by Leo Paper Products, Heshan, Guangdong
2 4 6 8 10 9 7 5 3

*For Ellsa, intrepid and adventurous*

*With special thanks to Julie Sykes*

# The Pony

Queen
Moonshine

Princess
Crystal

Princess
Cloud

Princess
Stardust

Princess
Honey

# Royal Family

King
Firestar

Prince
Jet

Prince
Comet

Prince
Storm

Cloud
Forest

Volcano

Wild Forest

Stableside
Castle

**Chevalia**

Horseshoe Hills

Savannah

Grasslands

Canter's Prep School

The Fields

Mane Street

Early one morning, just before dawn, two ponies stood in an ancient court-yard, looking sadly at a stone wall.

"In all my life this wall has never been empty. I can't believe that the horse-shoes have been taken—and just before Midsummer Day too," said the stallion.

He was a handsome animal—a copper-colored pony, with strong legs and bright eyes, dressed in a royal red sash.

The mare was a dainty yet majestic palomino with a golden coat and a pure white tail that fell to the ground like a waterfall.

She whinnied softly. "We don't have much time to find them all."

With growing sadness the two ponies watched the night fade away and the sun rise. When the first ray of sunlight spread into the courtyard it lit up the wall, showing the imprints where the golden horseshoes should have been hanging.

"Midsummer Day is the longest day of the year," said the stallion quietly. "It's the time when our ancient horseshoes must renew their magical energy. If the horseshoes are still missing in eight days, then by nightfall on the eighth day, their magic will fade and our beautiful island will be no more."

Sighing heavily, he touched his nose to his queen's.

"Only a miracle can save us now," he said.

The queen dipped her head, the diamonds on her crown sparkling in the early morning light.

"Have faith," she said gently. "I sense that a miracle is coming."

# Chapter 1

Pippa and Stardust were racing along a track in the Wild Forest. The trees grew close together, their thick branches keeping out all but a few thin rays of sunlight. The only sounds were Stardust's snorts and the muffled thudding of her hooves on the leaf-strewn path. Pippa hung on to Stardust's mane, concentrating on the trees, ducking to avoid low-hanging branches.

Suddenly a slanting ray of sunlight lit the path ahead, revealing a fallen tree. Pippa gasped. The trunk was massive, wider than the castle's moat and taller than the Whispering Wall. But Stardust was going too fast to stop, and there was nowhere to turn.

"Hold tight," she snorted.

She lengthened her stride and Pippa's heart thumped in her chest. They were going to jump it! With trembling hands, Pippa gripped Stardust's snowy white mane even tighter. Seconds later the princess pony jumped. Air rushed at Pippa's face and, as they flew upward, her stomach dipped. Images of a gnarled wooden trunk and a jumble of leafy branches jutting out in all directions

flashed before her eyes. Surely the tree was too huge for Stardust to clear?

As Pippa's stomach lurched, she heard a low, rhythmic noise in the air. What was that? It sounded like an enormous pair of beating wings.

"Stardust!" Pippa's breath caught in her throat. "Are we flying?"

"Yes!" Stardust's voice was shrill with excitement.

Pippa glanced down—and immediately wished she hadn't. The tall trees below looked like little broccoli florets from up here.

"Isn't this wonderful?" Stardust asked.

Pippa's legs tightened around her friend's flanks. Stardust felt reassuringly warm and solid. But how could she be flying? Pippa looked around, but suddenly Stardust dived, pitching Pippa forward and over her head. She tumbled through the air, the breath rushing out of her as the ground sped closer in a kaleidoscope of greens and browns.

*Thud!* Pippa landed on something soft. Her head jerked back and her eyes snapped open. Blinking in the gloomy light, she was surprised to see that she was in her own bed in Stardust's tower room at Stableside Castle.

"Oh, I was dreaming."

Pippa lay still while her racing heart slowed. It was ages before it began to beat normally. Across the room Princess Stardust snuffled and snored as she slept. Pippa watched the first light of dawn nudge at the tower window. It was followed by a familiar, rhythmic beat. Sitting up, Pippa turned her head toward the window to listen.

"Wings!" she said, leaping out of bed and running to the window.

Standing on her tiptoes, Pippa peeped outside. The sky was still dark,

with a few stars twinkling in the distance. The beating sound grew louder and more urgent. It reminded Pippa that there was something she ought to be doing. Her head swam as she struggled to remember what. It came to her in a rush. It was the day before Midsummer and three of the golden horseshoes were still missing.

"We have to find them!" she whispered to herself.

Pippa's hands curled into fists. She had been brought to the enchanted island of Chevalia, inhabited by talking ponies, to do a very special job. The eight golden horseshoes that were supposed to hang on the ancient Whispering Wall in the castle's courtyard had gone missing.

Without them, the magical island couldn't survive. Pippa had vowed to find the horseshoes and return them to their rightful home in time for their magical energy to be renewed on Midsummer Day.

She stared out, searching for the source of the flapping sound. It was louder now and was making the windowsill vibrate. Pippa looked out the window and up to the right.

"Peggy!"

A huge, silver horse hovered in the sky. Pippa hadn't seen Peggy since she helped them retrieve the first missing horseshoe from the foothills of the Volcano.

"Hello, Pippa," Peggy said warmly. "Congratulations. Triton and Rosella, the seahorses, tell me that you've found five of the missing horseshoes."

Shame and failure washed over Pippa. She felt she didn't deserve to be congratulated.

"But there are still three missing," she exclaimed.

"It's not Midsummer Day yet," Peggy said calmly. "Maybe I can help you find another horseshoe. Come here, child, and I'll take you on a tour of the island."

Pippa quickly dressed in the riding pants and horseshoe-patterned top that had appeared overnight especially for her, laid out neatly on a chair.

Peggy hovered next to the window, her feathery wings outstretched like a

glider. Reluctantly, Pippa moved closer. Surely Peggy didn't expect her to climb out of the window and onto her back? Pippa recoiled at the thought.

"I can't," she squeaked. "Stardust is still asleep. What if she wakes and finds me gone?"

"Stardust will be asleep for ages yet.

If you're scared of falling then don't be. I won't let you fall."

Pippa's chest tightened. Scared didn't even come close to how she felt. She was terrified of heights, even though she'd been learning to overcome her fear.

"Come," Peggy said, her eyes gently encouraging Pippa.

Pippa hesitated—it was hard not to trust Peggy. Staring at the flying horse's silver chest, she edged closer to the window.

"Don't look down," Peggy whispered.

Pippa concentrated on Peggy's wide back, which was as comfy-looking as a sofa. Reaching out of the window, she took a handful of mane.

"I can do this," she said firmly.

Her hands trembled like feathers in the wind as she climbed out onto the tower's windowsill. Her thudding heart made it almost impossible to breathe. Pippa paused to fill her lungs with the chilly dawn air. Then, with her eyes still on Peggy's back, she prepared herself for her next move.

"One, two, three," she whispered.

Quickly, before she could change her mind, Pippa scrambled onto Peggy's back. Once on it, she was too afraid to move. Peggy turned her head to nudge Pippa's foot with her nose.

"Well done," she neighed. "Now hold on tight."

A warm feeling spread upward from

Peggy's touch, filling Pippa with confidence. She could do this!

The sun was slowly rising behind them, bleeding red and gold across the dark sky, as Peggy soared up and over the Fields. Pippa's confidence gradually grew, until she was brave enough to look down. The island, surrounded by shimmering sea, was bathed in the soft gold glow of dawn. Even the dark Volcano was wrapped in a golden light that hung like a huge scarf around its craggy shoulders. Pippa searched for the peak of the Volcano but the wooded slopes disappeared into a summit of swirling mist. It was so beautiful that it made her heart sing.

"How could anyone want this to

disappear?" Pippa knew that she would do anything to save Chevalia.

Peggy skimmed over the treetops as she carefully swooped over the island. Pippa strained her eyes for the slightest flash of gold that could signal the missing horseshoes. As Peggy completed her first loop of the island, she climbed higher then hovered over the Fields. Far below, the tiny ponies, opening up their shops on Mane Street, reminded Pippa of the plastic ones in her brother's toy farmyard.

"Pippa." Peggy's voice was low and urgent, and it cut into her thoughts. "I want to ask you something. Take your time before you answer me. Would you like to go home, to the human world?"

A wave of homesickness washed over Pippa. When she stopped to think about it, she missed her family and home a great deal, even though they weren't missing her since Chevalia existed in a time bubble. Pippa could stay for as long as she liked while no time passed in her own world.

"I can't leave now," she said.

"It would be safer if you did. We might not find the remaining horse-shoes and I can't guarantee your safety."

Pippa felt as if her heart was being ripped in two. Suddenly she craved the safety of her family, but then again, how could she leave Stardust and Chevalia when they needed her help more than ever? The seconds ticked by. Wordlessly

Peggy glided in huge circles over the Fields.

"I made a promise to find the missing horseshoes," said Pippa finally. "I'm not going home until I do."

Peggy flapped her wings in double time.

"Pippa MacDonald, you are a true pony lover and a very special friend of Chevalia," she snorted.

# Chapter 2

Peggy flew over the island again, swooping even lower to help Pippa search for the missing horseshoes.

Keeping her eyes fixed on the passing landscape, Pippa asked her, "Why do you never land? Don't you get tired, staying in the air for so long?"

"I never used to get tired," said Peggy, "though recently my wings ache at night. But I can't land. The magic that lets me fly will vanish if I do and I'll become an ordinary pony."

"You'll never be ordinary," said Pippa.

Peggy's laughter sounded like music. "A very long time ago, when Chevalia was just a small volcanic island, I was an ordinary pony. I was lucky enough to make a very special friend, a scientist-magician named Nightingale. This pony had amazing powers and a brilliant mind. She discovered the magical gold buried in the volcanic rock. Nightingale realized the potential of that special gold, and she had it mounted on the Volcano. Over time the island grew larger and more magical, until it finally blossomed into the Chevalia that we know and love today. Nightingale had created a paradise, but that wasn't enough for her. She wanted to share it with ponies from around the world."

Pippa listened intently to Peggy's tale.

"Nightingale knew that some ponies were badly treated and had unhappy lives. It was those ponies that she wanted to come and live on Chevalia. So she invented a magic flying potion. The potion was so strong that it allowed the pony who drank it to fly forever, provided his or her hooves never touched the ground. And there was more—by drinking the potion, the pony could give the temporary gift of flight to any pony whose nose she rubbed. Nightingale asked me to drink the potion so that I could fly to the human world and rescue any unloved or mistreated pony who wanted a better life. The potion also kept me young, so for hundreds of years I flew around the world rescuing ponies in need and bringing them here to Chevalia. Once they arrive and their hooves touch the land, their wings vanish. Then they're free to live here in happiness, as every pony deserves."

"That's an amazing story," said Pippa. "What a wonderful job to have."

"Yes," Peggy sighed. "I've enjoyed every moment of it. But my wings are not as young as they were. When they ache, I dream of a cozy stable with a deep straw bed where I can rest my tired bones." She laughed softly. "But I still love to fly and help ponies in need. And as long as there are ponies to be helped I shall stay airborne."

"And I thought you flew because you were too special to walk on the ground," said Pippa.

Peggy laughed again. "No pony is too special to walk and talk with others."

"It's a big responsibility," Pippa said, full of admiration.

"I made a promise to Nightingale and to Chevalia," said Peggy.

Pippa nodded. She understood. She'd made a promise to help Chevalia too.

After they'd flown in silence for a while, Pippa said, "I have to go back to the castle soon. Stardust will worry if she wakes up and sees that I'm not there."

At once Peggy banked left then headed directly to Stableside Castle.

"Don't worry, Pippa. I'll continue searching for the horseshoes from the sky."

"And I'll keep searching too—with Stardust, of course," said Pippa.

When they reached Stardust's tower bedroom, Peggy came to a sharp halt, sending Pippa flying through the air. It was just like her dream, only this time she sailed through the tower window before landing with a thump on her bed. She caught a flash of Peggy's shiny hooves as she soared into the air, her silver tail streaming behind her.

"What's all the noise about?" groaned the waking Stardust. Rubbing her eyes with her hooves, she struggled up.

"You'll never guess where I've been," said Pippa. "Flying around the island on Peggy's back looking for horseshoes!"

"Liar, liar, tail's on fire," Stardust said

with a giggle. "You're still in bed, silly. You must have been dreaming."

"It wasn't a dream," Pippa insisted, but Stardust said nothing as she combed out her mane.

Pippa climbed out of bed and went over to the dresser to help her.

"We're running out of time. We've

got to continue searching for the remaining horseshoes."

"I agree," said Stardust. "But breakfast first. I'm starving. You know I can't work on an empty tummy."

Pippa let out a long sigh. She desperately wanted to continue her search, but she knew that Stardust was right.

"Breakfast first then," she agreed. "Let's hurry."

# Chapter 3

Pippa and Stardust made their way down the tower's spiral ramp to the dining room. Mrs. Steeplechase, the royal nanny, was striding up and down between the feeding troughs, snorting out orders to the prince and princess ponies.

"Let's go next to Cloud," Pippa said, concerned at how grumpy Stardust's sister looked.

The silver-gray pony was wearing a new tiara—gold, with pretty blue sapphires—instead of her usual wooden one that was decorated with acorns, but the sparking jewels couldn't hide her mood.

As Pippa and Stardust approached, Cloud tossed her head and walked away. Pippa's face fell.

"Don't mind her," Prince Comet said, closing the book he'd been reading while eating. Comet was a serious-looking pony with a dark brown coat and a thick, black mane and tail.

"Cloud can't help being grumpy. It's just the way she is," added Stardust.

Cloud stopped and turned back. "I'm not grumpy. I'm fed up. All everyone

talks about these days are the missing horseshoes and how Chevalia will fade away if they aren't found by tomorrow. Pah! Missing horseshoes, my hoof! It's just a silly story made up to frighten little ponies into behaving."

"It's not a story. It's a myth," said Comet.

"Same difference," argued Cloud. Irritably, she swished her long, gray tail as she hurried out of the dining room.

Comet shook his head. "It's not the same thing at all. Myths are so much more than make-believe—they originate from a popular belief. The ancient scrolls mention the power of the golden horseshoes. They're the key to Chevalia's survival."

Stardust took a mouthful of oats. She chewed them carefully before swallowing. "Cloud *is* always grumpy. Fact. That should be written in the ancient scrolls too."

Comet snorted with laughter.

"Has anyone tried to find out why she's grumpy?" asked Pippa.

33

Stardust stared at her. "There's no reason. It's just the way Cloud is," she replied.

"Well, maybe someone should ask her," Pippa said thoughtfully.

"Good luck with that. Don't be surprised if Cloud snaps your head off when you ask her." Stardust took another mouthful of oats.

Pippa reached for a bright red apple and polished it on her top.

"Is Cloud going to school now?" she asked.

"Not today," said Stardust. "That's one of the best things about the days leading up to Midsummer Day—we keep having holidays."

"But that doesn't mean you can

run wild for the day," snorted Mrs. Steeplechase.

Pippa jumped as the royal nanny appeared beside them. She listened patiently while Mrs. Steeplechase lectured them about behaving like proper princesses. When the nanny finally moved on, Pippa turned to Stardust.

"Wild!" she exclaimed. "I dreamed about the Wild Forest last night. We haven't searched there yet. Let's go there today."

Stardust's eyes sparkled with excitement. "Oooh! I love the Wild Forest. The ponies who live there have such fun. Maybe they'll let us play with them. After we've finished our search," she added quickly.

☆

After breakfast Pippa and Stardust rushed out of the castle.

"Hop on my back," said Stardust. "It's so much fun when you ride me."

Pippa jumped onto Stardust and the pony took off at a smart trot, her long,

white tail flowing behind her. They cantered across the wide Fields and plunged into the Wild Forest. Remembering her dream, Pippa kept a sharp lookout for fallen trees. Occasionally she'd see a group of wild ponies playing together. Once Stardust headed toward them, but the ponies ran away amid snorts of laughter.

"I'm not supposed to play in here," said Stardust. "Mrs. Steeplechase says it's not princess-like to mix with the wild ponies. She also worries about the mud. It sucks you in then swallows you up. But we're here to look for the horseshoes so that's all right."

Stardust trotted deeper into the forest. It was on the side of a steep hill and they were traveling downward so Pippa had to lean back. The last time she'd been here with Stardust they'd been going the other way. Riding downhill at speed was much trickier. Pippa didn't want to fall off and risk landing in the dangerous mud.

After riding for a while, Pippa noticed a tree with a trunk that was twisted like a question mark.

"Haven't we passed that tree once already?" she asked.

Stardust glanced at it as she trotted past. "I don't think so," she replied.

"Well, we've definitely passed that tree there," Pippa said, pointing to a bleached-white tree trunk that stuck up in the air like a giant knitting needle.

Stardust stopped to examine the branchless tree. "Hmmm," she said. "That's been hit by lightning. And you're right. We did pass it earlier." She turned in a slow circle then stopped.

Pippa stared at the trees crowding in on them. The Wild Forest was dark and gloomy. Fear prickled up her neck.

Stardust seemed uneasy too. Her muscles twitched and suddenly she shivered. Pippa hung on tight as Stardust trembled.

Very quietly Stardust whinnied, "I think we're lost."

# Chapter 4

Goosebumps formed on Pippa's arms, forcing the hairs to stand up in lines like soldiers. She breathed deeply, trying to squash the panic rising inside her.

"We're not totally lost," she said. Her voice came out in a squeak and she cleared her throat before continuing. "Uphill leads back to the Fields and downhill toward the beach."

"You're right," Stardust said, "but the forest is huge. We could walk for days without ever reaching the beach or the Fields."

A twig cracked behind her. Stardust turned around in time to see a silver-gray pony dashing through the forest. She was laughing so hard she didn't notice Pippa and Stardust.

"Catch me if you can!" she shouted, hopping over a fallen branch.

"Cloud?" Stardust said, her mouth open wide with shock.

"Coming to get you!" shrieked a familiar voice.

Stardust fell back, snorting with surprise, and Pippa blinked several times as a chestnut pony, wearing a satchel around her neck, chased after the silver-gray pony.

"That can't be Cinders." Pippa hesitated then added, "It is! It's Cinders and Cloud."

"They look like best friends," said Stardust.

She took off, chasing after them.

Pippa's wavy, dark hair streamed out behind her as Stardust ran through the forest. She could hardly believe it herself. Cinders never played with anyone. She was far too uppity for that, or so she'd thought. But here she was now, playing with Cloud in the Wild Forest.

"Look," Stardust snorted, suddenly changing direction.

Pippa's mouth fell open as a group of wild ponies ran past. They raced through the forest, leaping over fallen branches, jumping on top of tree stumps, and running up tree trunks to hurl themselves out of trees.

"That looks dangerous," gasped Pippa.

"It's called free-trotting," said

Stardust. "I've always wanted to try it but Mrs. Steeplechase won't let me. Look at that! Oh my goodness. They're never going to jump that ravine!"

The trees abruptly gave way to an enormous ravine with steep, craggy sides. Pippa felt nervous as Stardust trotted closer. It was a very long way down, and a river roared fiercely at the bottom. Stardust stopped closer to the edge than Pippa would have liked, but the free-trotting ponies were speeding up. Pippa covered her face with her hands, only managing to peer at the ponies through a gap in her fingers. There were loud snorts of laughter as, in groups of three, the wild ponies hurled themselves over the edge of the ravine. As the ponies jumped, their tails and manes streamed out like multi-colored flags in the wind.

Pippa couldn't breathe when she realized that Cloud and Cinders were jumping with them. Time seemed to stop as Cloud and Cinders launched themselves across the gaping chasm.

There were two loud thuds and thick clods of mud flew through the air. Pippa blinked, and when she looked again Cloud and Cinders were safely on the other side, blowing through their noses and laughing with the wild ponies.

"Awesome," she breathed.

Stardust danced on her hooves with excitement. "That was amazing. Did you see Cloud and Cinders jumping together? I'd love to try that," she added longingly.

"I bet they had lots of practice first," Pippa said anxiously.

Stardust giggled. "Don't worry. I'm not about to give it a go. That sort of jump must take ages to perfect. But how did Cloud and Cinders learn to do it?"

Stardust's eyes twinkled. "Unless that's what Cloud does when she goes off in a sulk. I bet she comes here to practice. No wonder she's so good—she's always going off in a huff!"

Stardust edged even closer to the ravine.

"Hi, Cloud," she called. "That was amazing."

Cloud turned around in surprise, and her face darkened with anger.

"Stardust!" she exclaimed. "Go away. This is *my* special place. Anyway, you're not allowed to play here."

# Chapter 5

Cinders turned back to her friend, her eyes full of suspicion.

"Cloud," she groaned, "what did you invite them for?"

"I didn't," Cloud snorted, annoyed. "They must have followed me here."

"We didn't follow you!" said Stardust. "Well, only a little bit. We came to the Wild Forest to look for the missing horseshoes, but we found you instead."

Cloud stomped her hoof. "Great! And now you're going to tell on me."

"No," exclaimed Stardust. "I'm not a tattletale!"

"We saw your free-trotting and it was incredible," Pippa said, changing the subject. "It must have taken you ages to learn how to do it."

"Not really," replied Cloud. "The main thing is confidence. If you're not scared to try, then it's really easy. The wild ponies are brilliant teachers. They're patient and kind, not like grumpy old Mrs. Steeplechase."

"The wild ponies sound amazing," Pippa agreed.

Cloud's eyes twinkled. "They're very good friends of mine," she said.

"Not everyone likes them but that's because they don't know them. You've got to look past the outside—just because ponies are scruffy that doesn't make them bad. My wild pony friends are caring and generous. And they like me for who I am. They're not interested in titles—no one cares if I'm a princess here. This is the only place in Chevalia where I can be my real self. Free-trotting is part of that. It makes me feel alive. It makes me feel like I can fly, and I love that."

"I love flying too," said Pippa. She didn't add that she'd flown with Peggy only that morning in case it sounded like she was boasting.

Cloud shyly dipped her head. "Would

you like to come free-trotting with me?"

"I'd love to," Pippa said, tempted to accept Cloud's invitation. "But we need to find the three missing horseshoes, and time is running out."

"The missing horseshoes!" Cloud sighed. "I'm still not sure I believe in all that."

"Neither do I," Cinders chipped in. "Mom says it's all a load of garbage."

"But what if it is true?" Pippa asked quietly.

Cloud scuffed a hoof on the ground. "That old Whispering Wall doesn't look right without the horseshoes. I suppose we could help you search for them, just to make it look normal again—not because I believe in all that 'horseshoe magic.'"

"It could be fun," Cinders agreed. "I bet the wild ponies would help us too."

"Would they?" asked Pippa. "That would be great. The more eyes the better."

Only Stardust looked doubtful. "I don't know," she said. "We're not really supposed to be here. Maybe we should go back now."

"But you're here now," called out a cheeky young chestnut pony with a white blaze. "And I've seen you and that girl here once before."

Stardust blushed bright red. "You're right. Pippa and I took a shortcut through the forest the day she arrived on Chevalia."

"We don't mind," said the wild pony. "You're welcome to come here anytime you like. My name's Clipper. I can teach you to free-trot if you like."

Stardust's eyes widened. "Really? I'd love that."

"Stand back then," said Clipper. "I'll jump back over the ravine so we're on the same side."

Led by Clipper, the wild ponies, Cloud, and Cinders jumped the ravine.

Cloud trotted over to Pippa. "Would you like to ride on me while Stardust learns how to free-trot?"

"Yes, thank you," said Pippa.

She slid from Stardust's back and jumped onto Cloud's. The older princess pony was taller and broader than Stardust, and Pippa almost didn't make it. Clinging on to Cloud's gray mane, she pulled herself on in an undignified scramble.

"Well done," Cinders said, helping

Pippa up with a friendly nudge to her foot.

"Missing horseshoes, here we come," Cloud whinnied.

Cloud set off at such a high speed it made Pippa's teeth snap like a crocodile's.

"You're so fast," she squealed.

"This is the one place I can let my mane down," said Cloud. "If I didn't have the Wild Forest to escape to I'd go absolutely mad with boredom. I hate living in the Royal Court with all its stuffy rules and traditions. Here in the Wild Forest everyone is equal. I don't have to keep curtsying, and I don't have to wear that stupid tiara."

Pippa ran her hand down Cloud's

neck, feeling the princess pony's muscles rippling as she leaped from one obstacle to the next. There were plenty of low-hanging branches to land on and tree stumps to jump over, but Pippa liked it best when Cloud trotted up the trunks to hurl herself out of the trees. It made her stomach flutter with excitement.

"This is fantastic," she yelled in Cloud's ear, making her buck for joy.

A long time later, they trotted into a clearing. Everyone slowed to catch their breath and cool down.

"Well done—you're a fast learner," Clipper told Stardust.

"Watch out," Cloud said, suddenly swerving left. "Mud."

Stardust bumped into Cinders, knocking her satchel. "Sorry," she apologized.

"No problem," Cinders said, shrugging off her satchel. "You've just reminded me I was supposed to get rid of this old thing for Mom."

The wild ponies trotted on, but Stardust and Cloud waited for Cinders.

"Why does the Baroness want you to throw her satchel in the mud?" Pippa asked, curious. "It doesn't look that old."

"Mom's even stricter than Mrs. Steeplechase," said Cinders. "You do what she says without questioning her."

Pippa stared at the satchel. Something was bothering her, but she wasn't sure what. Images of her previous adventures with Stardust flashed through her mind—the Night Mares, the mysterious hooded pony, and all the nasty comments Divine had made each time they were successful in their search.

"What's inside?" she asked suddenly.

"I don't know," said Cinders. "Like I said, you don't question Mom."

"May I have a look?"

Cinders hesitated then passed the satchel to Pippa. "Why not? Mom didn't tell me I couldn't show anyone."

The satchel was surprisingly heavy. Pippa felt all eyes watching her as she opened it up. As the flap fell back a flash of golden light blinded her. She blinked as she carefully opened the satchel wider.

"One—no, *two* of the missing horse-shoes," she exclaimed.

"No!" Cinders whinnied, the color draining from her face.

"Are you sure?" Stardust and Cloud crowded closer.

"I don't understand." Cinders had tears in her eyes. "Mom doesn't believe in the legend of the horseshoes, so why would she take them?"

"She almost had you bury them forever," Cloud said quietly.

There was a shrill neigh and a hooded pony crashed into the clearing. It thundered over to Pippa. She froze as the hooded pony tore the satchel out of her hands and threw it into the mud.

"Divine!" squeaked Stardust.

"Mom?" Cinders pushed the hood back from the pony's face.

"How could you?" shouted Pippa.

She lunged for the satchel. One moment it was floating in the mud but, just as she reached to save it, there was a loud sucking noise like water being pulled down a giant drain. The mud belched out one large, brown bubble then closed over the satchel, swallowing it whole.

The golden horseshoes were gone.

# Chapter 6

Pippa stared in horror at the powerful mud.

"Oh no!" neighed Stardust.

Pippa couldn't let Chevalia disappear with the satchel. "The horseshoes!" she cried, leaping into the mud.

"Pippa, no!" shrieked Stardust.

Pippa wasn't thinking clearly as she plunged her hands into the thick mud, her fingers searching for the satchel.

"I've got it," she called. "I've got the strap."

But the mud had hold of Pippa. The more she struggled to pull her hands out, the farther the mud sucked her down.

Pippa froze, not wanting to risk being pulled down even more.

"How stupid of me!" she muttered. How could she have been so reckless?

But she wasn't the only one not thinking. Cloud launched herself into the mud to help Pippa. Somehow they managed to pull the satchel free and toss it to Stardust.

Divine jumped forward. "Silly little girl," she shouted. "This isn't your battle. Why can't you mind your own business and go back to where you came

from?" She snatched the satchel from under Stardust's nose and ran away into the forest.

Cloud and Pippa were sinking fast. "Use my back as a stepping stone to get to solid land," Cloud shouted.

Using all her strength, Pippa reached out for a clump of Cloud's mane and pulled herself onto her back. The added weight made Cloud sink faster. Quickly Pippa jumped for dry ground, landing with a squish. Mud splattered from her feet, covering Stardust and Cinders. For once Cinders didn't seem to mind she was dirty. She raced to the nearest tree and began to gnaw at the lowest branch with her teeth.

"Help me," she grunted.

Pippa reached her first, closely followed by Stardust. They wiggled the branch up and down while Cinders continued to chew on it. At last it snapped free.

"Easy now," Cinders said, as she guided it back to the mud. She laid the branch over the mud like a bridge.

"Hold on to the end," she called to Cloud.

Cloud held on to the branch with her mouth.

"Ready, everyone? On the count of three, pull," said Cinders.

Pippa's fingers gripped the branch tightly. As everyone pulled, the bark cut into her hand. She winced but never let go even though it felt like her arm was going to be pulled off. The drag of the mud made Cloud feel ten times heavier than she really was. Sweat trickled down Pippa's face. Gritting her teeth, she pulled harder. There was a crack like thunder and the branch snapped. Pippa fell backward, and Stardust and Cinders almost fell over too. Cloud was sinking even farther into the mud.

Stardust bolted to the edge of the forest, where long vines trailed from the trees. Selecting the strongest-looking vine, she broke it off and brought it back to the mud.

"Catch," she said, throwing one end to Cloud.

The vine fell short. Stardust reeled it in and threw it again. By now Cloud's back had disappeared and the mud was creeping up her neck. Pippa fought back tears. She couldn't let anything happen to Cloud, especially as the pony had just saved her life.

"Let me," she said, taking the vine from Stardust.

Pippa took a deep breath as she aimed. The vine snaked across the mud and landed at Cloud's head. Gratefully Cloud caught it in her teeth.

"Pull," called Pippa. "Harder."

But it was no use. Cloud was stuck— and was sinking even deeper. She was going to disappear into the mud, and it was all Pippa's fault.

Suddenly, a familiar, rhythmic noise sounded in the air. Pippa glanced up.

"Peggy," she gasped.

The sun flashed on Peggy's silvery wings, filling Pippa with hope, as the flying horse dived for Cloud. She hovered above the ground and rubbed noses with the terrified pony. The mud began to shake and bubble. Pippa

stared in amazement as a set of wings broke through the surface of the mud.

"You've given Cloud wings to fly," she breathed.

"Yes," Peggy neighed. "I'm allowed to use my magic to help any pony in trouble, even if they already live here on Chevalia."

Cloud's eyes widened in surprise and at once she began flapping her wings, causing the mud to bubble like lava.

"Harder," Pippa encouraged her.

Cloud's new wings soon found a rhythm. Mud sprayed off her in all directions, splattering everyone. Then, with an enormous *pop*, Cloud burst free.

"Hooray," cheered Pippa.

Cloud rose into the air but the mud

on her wings was making her fly crook-edly. She rolled toward Peggy, slapping her with a muddy wing. Caught off-balance, Peggy fell backward and landed on the ground. There was a loud *clap* and a flash of brilliant green light. Silence followed.

Everyone stared at Peggy. Her wings

had disappeared, leaving her as a pretty, silver-colored pony.

Cloud came over, squealing in horror. "What have I done? I'm so sorry. How can you ever forgive me?"

A slow smile spread across Peggy's face. "The power is yours now, Cloud. I bestow upon you the magical gift of flight. Use it wisely. There are many ponies in the human world who need help. Go and seek them out, and, by rubbing noses with them like I did to you, allow them to fly so that they may come here to the safety of Chevalia."

"If there still is a Chevalia," Stardust burst out. "Divine has run off with two of the horseshoes."

Cloud hovered above Peggy.

"Are you sure that's what you want?" Cloud asked. "I could rub noses with you and transfer the power back."

Peggy closed her eyes. "I've loved my job. But I've done it for hundreds of years, and lately I've grown tired. It's time to step down and let someone younger take my place—if you want to, that is?"

Cloud's silver-gray chest swelled with pride. "I do. I want it more than anything."

"Then the power is yours," said Peggy. "And will be for as long as you stay in the air."

Stardust was becoming impatient. "But what about the horseshoes?" she shouted.

"Can I make them fly?" Cloud asked, nodding at Stardust and Cinders.

Peggy smiled and whispered, "The power is yours."

Cloud flew to Stardust. Keeping her hooves above the ground, she rubbed noses with her sister. There was a crack and a flash of light. Stardust gasped.

"I've got wings!"

"Me too," Cinders cried, as Cloud rubbed noses with her friend.

"Hurry, Pippa! Climb on my back." Stardust hovered as low as she dared without touching the ground.

Pippa reached for a handful of mane and pulled herself up on Stardust's back.

"Ready?" asked Stardust.

"Let's fly," Pippa agreed.

Stardust flapped her enormous, feathery wings. The breeze fanned Pippa's face and lifted her hair as they rose into the air. Cloud and Cinders flew up next to them, weaving through the branches until they were flying above the trees.

"There's Mom," Cinders said, pointing

with one of her hooves to a tiny pony who was racing beneath them through the forest.

"After her," cried Pippa.

Side by side, the three ponies flew after Divine.

# Chapter 7

The Baroness galloped through the forest. She kept glancing upward as she weaved through the trees. The satchel swung wildly from her mouth. It got snagged on a branch, but Divine yanked it free and galloped on.

"Hurry," urged Pippa. "She's getting away."

Stardust's wings beat faster, fanning cold air at Pippa and making her eyes tear.

Divine burst from the Wild Forest and onto the vast green Fields. Head down, she galloped straight across it. As she reached the other side, she darted toward a bush and disappeared down a hidden path.

"Where's she going?" Cloud wondered.

"That's a secret path to the Volcano," Cinders said as she flew after her mother, her wings creaking, her muscles straining with the effort.

"The Volcano? But why would she go there?" asked Stardust.

The flying ponies were finally gaining on Divine.

"Stop her," shouted Cloud.

As one, the trio of flying ponies

swooped in on Divine. Stardust and Cloud flew on either side of Divine while Cinders floated down in front of her mother.

With the ground approaching, Cloud called frantically, "Hooves up. Don't touch the ground."

Pippa was breathless with excitement and fear. Her knees gripped Stardust's flanks and her fingers were tightly wrapped around Stardust's mane.

Cinders hovered in front of Divine. "Stop!" she called. "Where are you taking the horseshoes?"

Divine tossed her head. "Get out of my way, foal."

"Please, Mom," begged Cinders. "Give the horseshoes back. No one needs to know it was you who took them."

"Never." Divine's eyes rolled wildly, showing their whites. "I'm taking the horseshoes home, where they belong."

"They belong on the Whispering Wall," said Pippa.

Divine laughed hysterically. Suddenly she rose up, and, shoving her face at Cloud, she rubbed noses with her. There was a loud crack and a blinding flash of light. Black dots swam in front of Pippa's eyes, and she rapidly blinked them away. A breeze fanned her face. Squinting at Divine, she saw that the pony was sprouting an enormous pair of chestnut-brown wings.

"No," Pippa breathed, an icy feeling shivering down her spine.

A wicked smile lit Divine's face. Experimentally at first, she flapped her wings. Her confidence grew as they lifted her into the air.

"The time has come," she whinnied, her shrill voice echoing weirdly as she flew higher above the narrow path, "to return this island to its original form!"

Pippa clenched Stardust's mane, fighting back tears, as Divine flew away triumphantly, the satchel swinging from her mouth.

"After her!" ordered Pippa.

"Yes, hurry," said Cloud.

In a whir of wings, the three ponies gave chase. Stardust's huge, white wings clapped together as she climbed higher. Pippa could hardly breathe. The ground whizzed away from her in a blurred mix of greens, browns, and sparkling blue sea. They flew over Stableside Castle, the eight flags fluttering from each of its toy-sized towers. Soaring after Divine was like playing a crazy game of tag. Each time Stardust, Cloud, and Cinders drew closer, Divine would suddenly change direction.

"Hold tight," Stardust shrieked, shooting left. Pippa slid right and barely held on.

Soon after that, Pippa began to cough. Smoke and ash hung in the air, tickling her nose and sticking to the back of her throat.

"We're almost at the top of the Volcano," Stardust said, coughing.

Pippa stared ahead as a tall cone of black rock rose from the tip of a cloud. Smoke belched from the Volcano. Sweat trickled down her face. She coughed again, clutching Stardust's mane as she used her other arm to cover her mouth.

Then, all at once, she had an idea.

"Cinders, Cloud," she whispered urgently. "Make Divine go higher."

Unquestioningly Cloud and Cinders did as she asked, but when Stardust tried to follow Pippa stopped her.

"Hide in the cloud above," she whispered.

Stardust's ears flickered quizzically as she followed Pippa's instruction.

When the misty cloud surrounded them, Pippa called out again, "There's Divine—below us. Can you fly down and surprise her?"

"I certainly can," Stardust said, dropping straight down.

Pippa kept her eyes on Divine's broad back as they flew down toward her. A dangerous plan was forming in her head. Pippa didn't share it with Stardust in case the pony tried to stop her.

"Three, two, one," she counted, then leaped from Stardust onto Divine.

"Pippa!" Stardust cried in horror.

Pippa smiled grimly as she landed on Divine's back.

"Get off, you horrible little girl!" Divine bucked wildly, twisting in the air to try and unseat Pippa.

With a viselike grip, Pippa hung on to Divine's mane with one hand as she swung down to grab the satchel with the other. Taken by surprise, Divine let it go. Pippa threw the strap over her head, then leaped onto Cloud's back—the

princess pony had been flying next to them. Pippa was trembling like crazy, but she'd made it!

"Noooo!" shrieked Divine. She reached for the satchel, but Pippa held it high above her head. Divine lunged again. Pippa swung the satchel around to the other side. Divine snapped her teeth, but Pippa ducked.

Cloud darted away, startling Divine, who continued flying, almost slamming straight into the side of the Volcano. With an angry screech, she folded her wings back, sticking out her hooves as she skidded to a halt. She was still traveling too fast. Her hooves pedaled the air and, with a crunch, she plowed into the side of the Volcano. There was a loud *pop*.

"Aaaaarghh!" Divine's furious screams rang out as her wings vanished.

Cinders flew behind Divine, holding her wings outward and upward to slow down. Pippa winced, but Cinders managed to stop, her hooves barely an inch from the ground. Sweat dripped from her heaving sides.

"That was close," she panted. "I thought I was going to crash into the Volcano."

"You silly little foal," spat Divine. "How could you betray me like this?"

"No, Mom," Cinders said, her voice trembling. "How could you betray Chevalia?"

"You don't understand," said Divine, her voice husky with regret. "Chevalia needs a change. But it isn't over yet."

The words hung in the air. Divine snorted then, turning around, she cantered up the Volcano's steep slope. Pippa watched until her large chestnut body was totally swallowed up by the misty cloud at the summit. Slowly she opened the satchel and removed the two golden horseshoes. As she held them up, the horseshoes glittered brightly, their magic spreading hope among the three ponies hovering in the air.

Stardust bucked triumphantly. "We've almost done it," she exclaimed.

"Almost," Pippa breathed. "But Divine is right. It's not over yet. There's still one horseshoe missing."

# Chapter 8

Pippa held the horseshoes tightly as Stardust, Cloud, and Cinders flew back to the castle. They made a magnificent sight, flying like three huge birds over the island. Word soon spread and by the time they approached the castle, a crowd was waiting to greet them. The ponarazzi were there, pushing to the front of the crowd. Flying in a V-shape, the ponies soared over the clicking cameras, dipping their wings in salute as they flew onto the castle grounds. Pippa blinked furiously—the pop and flash of the ponarazzi cameras were as irritating as a cloud of gnats.

Stardust and Cinders landed in the Royal Courtyard to a gasp of admiration from the watching crowd. There was a loud crack as their hooves touched down. In a flash of light their wings vanished.

Stardust sighed happily. "That was such fun."

Cloud hovered several inches above the ground as everyone made their way to Queen Moonshine, King Firestar, and Peggy, who was wearing a new sash of deep green and a jade-studded tiara.

Stardust and Cinders curtsied so low their forelegs almost touched the rough stone floor.

"Welcome back," Queen Moonshine said, her voice as rich as warm honey.

Pippa sneaked a glance at the queen. She was looking even more beautiful than ever. Her long mane and tail flowed to the ground in a snow-white waterfall. Her golden coat shone from hours of grooming, and her hooves were painted with a pearly hoof gloss. In contrast, Peggy's gray coat was flecked with the white hairs of old age. Her muzzle was wrinkled and her hooves worn. She looked so much older than when Pippa had left her in the forest.

"You've been very brave," the queen said, looking first at Pippa, then Stardust, Cinders, and Cloud. "Peggy has told me everything—how you ventured into the Wild Forest then chased the Night Mares to retrieve two of the missing horseshoes."

Night Mares? Pippa opened her mouth to protest, but she felt Peggy's gaze boring into her. Peggy shook her head ever so slightly. Pippa snapped her mouth shut. Peggy looked away and Pippa was left wondering if perhaps she'd imagined the headshake. But Stardust, Cinders, and Cloud didn't correct Peggy either so Pippa decided she hadn't imagined it and remained silent.

"You may come down," Queen

Moonshine told Cloud. "The danger is over."

Cloud stayed in the air.

A *tsk* rang out behind her. The watching ponies parted as Mrs. Steeplechase pushed her way to the front.

"Your mother said to come down," the royal nanny said forcefully. "Hovering in the air isn't appropriate for a young princess."

Cloud smiled politely. "Peggy has lost her wings." She paused, her silence hanging in the air. "Chevalia needs a new flying pony—someone to go to the human world to save the neglected ponies. Someone to lead them to Chevalia, where they can be happy and free."

Mrs. Steeplechase inhaled sharply, but Queen Moonshine nodded, her eyes soft with understanding.

"Do you wish to take Peggy's place?" she asked.

"Yes." Cloud nodded fiercely. "More than anything."

"Then the role is yours with my blessing," said the queen. A tear formed in her eye and she blinked it away. "Just remember to come back and visit us often."

"I will." Cloud darted forward as if to nuzzle her mother with her nose, then quickly shied away.

Stardust and Cinders giggled, and even Pippa managed a smile at the thought of the queen suddenly sprouting wings. The smile faded quickly, though, as she stared at the two horseshoes weighing heavily in her hand. There was still one horseshoe to find. Without it there would be no refuge for any ponies on Chevalia.

As if hearing her thoughts, Stardust burst out, "There's only one day left to find the last horseshoe if Chevalia is to survive."

Murmurs of shock rippled through the watching ponies.

"No!" exclaimed Pippa. "It won't come to that. I won't let it. We *will* find the final horseshoe. I promise it'll be back on the Whispering Wall before sundown on Midsummer Day."

A cheer rose from the crowd. Pippa

felt sick with fear, but she forced herself to smile back.

"And now," said King Firestar, "let's hang the horseshoes in their rightful place on the Whispering Wall."

He nodded to Pippa but, instead of stepping forward herself, she waved Cloud closer.

"You should do this," Pippa said, handing her the horseshoes.

Cloud blushed, but her protests were drowned out by the cheering crowd.

"Cloud, Cloud, Cloud," they chanted.

Shyly, Cloud took the horseshoes from Pippa and flew to the wall. As the rays from the sun shone on the ancient stonework, Cloud hung the horseshoes back where they belonged. She flew

backward as they fizzled and flashed
with magic.

The ponies cheered and stomped
their hooves. Cloud tossed her head
then soared upward. She circled the
Royal Courtyard once then flew
away.

Pippa realized she was holding her

breath. Letting it out, she turned to Stardust and hugged her tightly.

"We can do this," she vowed.

"We can," Stardust neighed. "For the love of Chevalia, we can."

# Chevalia Now!

## EXCLUSIVE INTERVIEW WITH PEGGY

by Tulip Inkhoof

After a lifetime in the air, Peggy has given up her wings and passed them—and the responsibility that comes with them—to none other than Princess Cloud, third in line to the throne of Chevalia. The mysterious former winged horse shared her secrets with me as she curled up on a straw sofa and sipped apple-spice tea.

☆ **TI (Tulip Inkhoof):** Peggy, can you please tell our readers how you came to be a winged horse?

☆ **P (Peggy):** It was a long, long time ago, my dear—back then, Chevalia wasn't much more than a volcanic rock in the sea. My friend Nightingale was a brilliant scientist-magician. She found a way to increase the island's size and magic, and she was determined to make it a safe haven for ponies from the human world who were treated poorly. Nightingale developed a

magic flying
potion that
gave me
wings, and
for hundreds
and hundreds
of years I flew
all over the
human world, rescuing
neglected ponies and bringing them here.

☆ **TI:** Why haven't we been able to meet you until now?

☆ **P:** Well, Tulip, an unfortunate side effect of Nightingale's potion was that I couldn't set my hooves on land. If I had, I'd have lost my wings. That was something I had to sacrifice in order to help other ponies.

☆ **TI:** Did that make you sad?

3

☆ **P:** Yes and no. I've always taken pleasure in seeing the rescued ponies have long, fun-filled lives on Chevalia. In fact, I brought your great-great-grandmare to this island—I can still remember it like it was yesterday. She was curious like you, but treated poorly in the human world. I found her tied to a post in a busy, crowded town. When I rubbed noses with her, she grew wings like mine, although hers were temporary, and together we flew to Chevalia, where she touched down and started a new life. It fills my heart with joy to know that I've helped achieve Nightingale's dream for Chevalia. But, I must admit, occasionally I felt a small pang of envy when I watched ponies

4

galloping and frolicking. Sometimes I wished I could just land and have a good canter myself.

☆ **TI:** And now you can!

☆ **P:** Yes, that's right. Another pony—a very brave pony—has taken on the wings of responsibility.

☆ **TI:** So it's true? You can confirm that Princess Cloud has become the new Peggy?

☆ **P:** Cloud is the new Cloud! She is her own pony, and I'm sure she'll fulfill her duties admirably.

☆ **TI:** But she's always been the grumpiest of the Royal Ponies!

5

**P:** I believe there's good in all ponies, and I suspect that Cloud has been misunderstood by some of us. She craves a life of adventure and travel. Being cooped up in Stableside Castle, with its many rules, was too strict for such a life-loving pony.

**TI:** I've never thought about it like that.

**P:** You never truly know a pony until you step into their horseshoes, young Tulip Inkhoof.

**TI:** And please tell us how you met Pippa MacDonald. I understand that you helped her retrieve the first magical horseshoe?

☆ **P:** Yes, I noticed that Pippa and Stardust were searching for something in the foothills of the Volcano, and I spotted something sparkly on a ledge. Luckily Pippa realized that I was trying to point it out to them.

☆ **TI:** You've gotten to know Pippa over the past few days, haven't you? Can you offer us any insights about her?

☆ **P:** Pippa is very loyal to her friends and those in need. I've been very impressed with her, especially this morning when I told her that she was free to return home if she wanted and that it would be safer for her there. She chose to stay and honor her promise to help Chevalia. The island needs bravery like hers now more than ever.

☆ **TI:** Well, Peggy, thank you so much for taking the time to talk to us. I hope you're enjoying being back on solid ground!

It's finally Midsummer Day.
Will Pippa and Princess Stardust
find the last golden horseshoe
in time to save Chevalia?

DON'T MISS THEIR NEXT ADVENTURE
IN THE MOST DANGEROUS PART OF
THE ISLAND—THE VOLCANO!

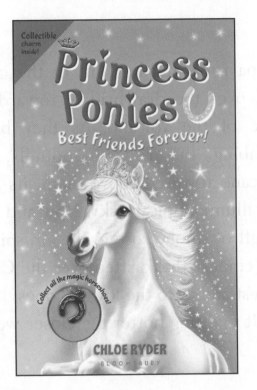

Turn the page to read a sneak peek . . .

Pippa rode Stardust out of the castle and over the drawbridge, toward the base of the Volcano. As they began climbing the rugged foothills, the Volcano towered above them, its fiery top illuminating the sky. Now and then a puff of smoke rose in the air, spilling red cinders that drifted over the Cloud Forest and onto the lower slopes.

"It's getting hotter the closer we get

to the Volcano," Stardust said, stopping to catch her breath.

"I'll walk," Pippa said, starting to slide from Stardust's back.

"No," the princess pony said quickly. "I like it when you ride on me. It feels right."

She shied, narrowly avoiding a cloud of sparks as they shot to the ground.

"Even the Volcano feels angry. Maybe this really is the end for Chevalia."

"Never," Pippa said forcefully.

They continued in silence and soon they entered the mysterious Cloud Forest, home to the secretive unicorns. The forest felt cool and fresh. Pippa loved the way the sunlight filtered through the ancient trees, dotting the path with golden puddles of light. Stardust slowed down, weaving a careful path through the forest to avoid the enormous vines that trailed from branches like long snakes. They were over halfway through the forest when the hairs on Pippa's neck rose and her arms tingled with goosebumps. Convinced she was being watched, she looked around.

"What's wrong?" asked Stardust.

The forest around them was silent and still. As they stared into the cloudy gloom suddenly something jumped from a tree and stood on the path ahead. Stardust flinched then burst out laughing.

"Misty!" she cried.

Pippa appreciated once more just

how similar Misty was to Stardust. The unicorn was almost identical to her friend, from the tilt of her head to the tip of her snow-white tail. The only differences were the pretty golden horn on the top of Misty's head and their size—Misty was the size of a large dog.

"Hello!" Misty's musical voice bubbled with excitement. "Is it time already? Have you come to get us for the Midsummer Concert?"

Stardust shook her head sadly.

"I'm sorry, Misty, but there might not be a concert now. One of the horseshoes is still missing."

"No!" Misty gasped. "But it's Midsummer Day."

"That's why we're here. We're on our way to the Volcano—we think the horseshoe could be hidden there," Pippa said.